Shh!
Can you
keep a secret?

You're about to meet the
Ballet Bunnies, who live hidden at
Millie's ballet school.

Are you ready?

Tiptoe this
way. . . .

Meet the
Ballet Bunnies

Dolly

Fifi

You'll never meet a bunny who loves to dance as much as Dolly.

If you're in trouble, Fifi is always ready to lend a helping paw!

Pod

Pod loves to build
things out of the bits
and pieces he finds. He
also loves his tutu!

Trixie

Yawn! When she's
not dancing, Trixie
likes curling up and
having a nice snooze.

For Ockie

Text copyright © 2020 by Swapna Reddy
Cover art and interior illustrations copyright © 2020 by Binny Talib

All rights reserved. Published in the United States by Random House Children's Books, a division of Penguin Random House LLC, New York. Originally published in paperback as *Millie's Birthday* by Oxford University Press, Oxford, in 2020.

Random House and the colophon are registered trademarks and A Stepping Stone Book and the colophon are trademarks of Penguin Random House LLC.

Visit us on the Web!
rhcbooks.com

Educators and librarians, for a variety of teaching tools, visit us at
RHTeachersLibrarians.com

Library of Congress Cataloging-in-Publication Data is available upon request.
ISBN 978-0-593-30569-0 (pbk.) — ISBN 978-0-593-30570-6 (lib. bdg.) —
ISBN 978-0-593-30571-3 (ebook)

MANUFACTURED IN CHINA
10 9 8 7 6 5 4 3 2

First American Edition 2021

This book has been officially leveled by using the
F&P Text Level Gradient™ Leveling System.

Ballet Bunnies

Ballerina Birthday

By Swapna Reddy

Illustrated by Binny Talib

A STEPPING STONE BOOK™

Random House New York

Chapter 1

"Wheeeeee!" Dolly whirled around the empty ballet studio. She pushed forgotten ballet slippers across the floor to Fifi, who dropped them in the lost and found box.

Millie smiled. It was the last day of

class at Miss Luisa's School of Dance before the holidays, and she had volunteered to tidy up the ballet studio until Mom came to pick her up. Miss Luisa had praised Millie for being such a good team player, but Millie had her own reasons to want to stay behind in the empty studio alone. Four

ballet-dancing, bunny-shaped reasons.

While Dolly did pirouettes, Pod helped Millie gather up the tutus the children had used during class. Trixie, the fourth and tiniest of Millie's ballet-bunny friends, slept soundly in the warm pocket of Millie's hoodie.

The Ballet Bunnies lived secretly in the school, and with no one but Millie in the studio they were free to dance (and sleep) there in the open.

"I'm going to miss you all during the holidays," Millie said, as she held Trixie safely in her pocket.

"We're going to miss you too," Fifi replied. She and Dolly pushed away the lost and found box and hopped over to join Millie and Pod.

"What are you going to do over the holidays?" Dolly asked.

Millie blushed. "Well, it's my birthday next week."

Pod, Fifi, and Dolly leapt up high and landed on Millie's shoulders to give her the warmest birthday nuzzles.

"Why didn't you tell us?" Fifi exclaimed. "Are you having a party?"

Millie nodded. "Mom is throwing me a big ballet birthday party next week," she said.

"How wonderful," Dolly squealed.

Pod looked thoughtfully at Millie as Dolly squeaked excitedly about how much she loved parties.

"Is everything okay, Millie?" Pod asked gently.

Millie sighed. "I was really happy when Mom told me about the party, but now I'm a bit worried about so many people coming to our house."

"But that's the best part!" Dolly said. "Everyone is there to celebrate you."

The bunnies hopped off Millie's shoulders as she slumped down to the ground. They gathered close around her.

"I get a funny, whirly feeling in my tummy when I think about everyone coming to the party," said Millie. "It feels like the inside of me is spinning too fast on a ride at the fairground."

Fifi and Dolly fell silent as Pod hopped even closer. "I understand, Millie," he said. "Sometimes all the noise and attention can be overwhelming."

Millie gazed down at the little bunny and scooped him and the other bunnies up. "I wish you could all come home with me for the holidays," she said. "I would feel much better about the party if you bunnies were there."

"I wish we could too," Fifi agreed.

Millie thought for a moment. "Well, why can't you?" She leapt up and then set the bunnies down, her eyes bright and excited. "You could stay in my room, and we could dance and play all day. And then you could come to my party too."

"Yes!" Dolly shrieked. "Great idea."

"Oh, bunny fluff," Fifi said slowly. "What if someone like Millie's mom sees us? Do you think we can stay hidden for that long?"

Before Millie could answer, Trixie's tiny face poked out from Millie's pocket.

"Of course we can!" she said.

Chapter 2

Taking the bunnies home in her bag was going to be tricky. They were far too heavy for Millie to be able to skip all the way home the way she usually did with Mom. And if she didn't skip, Mom might start asking questions.

So Millie kept Trixie tucked away in her pocket, while Dolly snuck into Millie's bag. "We can follow behind and keep out of sight," Pod and Fifi had agreed.

Millie kept Mom distracted on the way home, asking her questions about her day and sharing stories from the last ballet class. Just a few doors away from their house,

Mom stopped suddenly and spun around to look behind them. Millie turned to see that Fifi and Pod had darted behind a nearby tree trunk to stand as still as statues.

"Mom?" Millie started. She bounced nervously from foot to foot and held on to Trixie a little tighter.

Mom shook her head and turned back. "I thought someone was behind us." Mom shrugged and continued skipping beside Millie all the way to their front door.

◉ ✳ ◉

"That was close!" Dolly said. She scrambled out of Millie's bag the moment the four bunnies were safely in Millie's bedroom.

Pod picked out a leaf from his fur. "I told you we should have hidden behind that mailbox, Fifi."

"Oh, bunny fluff," Fifi said dismissively. "We're all here now, aren't we?"

She bounced up and down on Millie's bed before lying back in the soft sheets. "This is going to be the best bunny holiday ever," she said, grinning at the others.

Trixie yawned and her nose twitched as Millie placed her carefully down by her musical jewelry box. The little bunny popped open the lid to see the tiny ballerina inside begin to rotate to the tune from the box. Fifi, Pod, and Dolly giggled with glee, and together all four bunnies pirouetted around the box in time with the twinkly melody.

"Oh!" Fifi gasped. "Who is that?"

She stood motionless with one paw pointing in front of her.

Millie smiled and picked up the pretty ballerina doll Fifi was looking at. The china doll was dressed in a pink silk ballet dress and had miniature ivory ballet slippers on her feet. Her dark hair was pulled back in a bun, and a yellow satin flower was pinned behind her ear.

Carefully holding the doll, Millie sat down on her bed to show it to the bunnies.

"She was my granny's when she was a little girl," Millie said. "Granny named her Sylvie after a famous dancer she knew."

Millie reached up to a shelf above her

bed and pulled down a little blue hat with bunny ears made out of paper.

"I made this for Sylvie," she said as she placed the hat on Sylvie's head.

"Now she looks like one of us!" Fifi exclaimed.

Dolly hopped closer and gently ruffled the hem of Sylvie's dress. As the dress tumbled back into place, the pink fabric shimmered.

"She's so special," Dolly whispered.

"She's the most special thing I have." Millie smiled. But her smile quickly gave way to a frown. "Mom is always telling me to be more careful with Sylvie. I keep

leaving her around the house, but really she needs to stay where she will be safe."

Millie then put Sylvie back on her shelf.

"I know," Dolly said. "Let's show Sylvie our *pliés*."

Millie lined up alongside the bunnies

as they turned out their heels and curtsied into a *plié*.

"And now, *relevé*," Dolly said, sounding just like Miss Luisa, the ballet teacher.

Millie and the bunnies laughed but rose up on their tiptoes just as Dolly had asked.

"And now *disco pirouettes*!" Dolly cried.

Millie fell back onto her bed, laughing really hard as Dolly wiggled her bottom and twirled in circles.

"What exactly is going on in here?"

Chapter 3

Millie spun around to see Mom in the doorway.

"Well?" Mom demanded.

"I . . . ," Millie stammered. "I can explain."

Millie could feel her heart pounding hard in her chest. She couldn't believe it. The bunnies had been discovered *already*.

Perhaps Mom would understand if she got to know the Ballet Bunnies? she thought. In any case, Millie had no choice now but to introduce them. She turned to pick up her friends.

But they had all disappeared!

Millie's eyes darted around her room. Where had they gone?

"Well?" Mom said, tapping her foot.

Millie was just going to have to tell her the truth.

She opened her mouth to explain, but Mom interrupted her.

"Are you going to explain why you were playing *without* me?" Mom said. But a smile broke across her face.

Millie was confused. Had Mom really not seen Dolly, Fifi, Trixie, and Pod?

Mom plopped down onto Millie's bed and picked up a teddy bear. "So, what are we playing?"

"I *was* playing hide-and-seek with my toys," Millie said quickly, distracted as she searched the room for the bunnies.

They weren't in the toy box. They weren't under her pillow. They weren't hidden between her books. And they weren't burrowed in her rolls of ribbons.

Suddenly, the tiniest of twitches caught her eye. There, in her pile of teddy bears! One bunny was wearing a borrowed teddy hat. One wore a pair of teddy glasses.

Another was wrapped in a teddy scarf. The fourth bunny was snoozing on top of a fluffy unicorn.

Millie put her hand over her mouth to stop herself from laughing.

"It's almost time for dinner, so I'm not sure we can play a *whole* game of hide-and-seek," Mom said. "How about we play after dinner?"

Millie nodded and threw herself into Mom's arms to shield the bunnies from view.

"I can't believe you are going to be a whole year older next week," Mom said, kissing Millie on the forehead. "Are you still excited about your party?"

Millie sat in Mom's lap as all her worries about the party came back. Then her foot brushed a teddy bear on the floor, and she

remembered her four little bunny friends, who'd promised to help her through the next week.

"Yes, Mom." She nodded. "I can't wait for the party."

Mom smiled, and as soon as she'd headed back downstairs, Dolly, Fifi, Pod, and Trixie hopped out of their hiding spots.

"Can we still come to your party?" Dolly asked hopefully.

"Ooh, I hope so!" Fifi added.

Millie scooped up Pod and grinned at the others.

"I couldn't have a party without all of you!" she said.

Chapter 4

The next week was filled with fun and dancing. One day, Millie took the bunnies for a bicycle ride, tucking them into the basket on the front of her bike. Another day, they all pirouetted around the garden and formed a conga line across her bedroom. And at bedtime every night,

Millie read Fifi, Dolly, Pod, and Trixie stories about ballerina ponies and tap-dancing kangaroos.

The bunnies had been great at keeping out of sight. Whenever Millie's mom appeared, they would either dart behind Millie's stash of comics or burrow under her comforter in the nick of time. Trixie even managed to hide on top of one of Mom's fluffy slippers without her noticing!

With all the holiday fun she was having, Millie hadn't had a chance to think about how nervous she was about her party. Now she gazed around the garden. There was a long table covered with a blue polka-dot tablecloth and filled with star-shaped sandwiches, pink wafer cookies, purple fairy cakes with sprinkles, and a strawberry-flavored cake topped with ballet shoes made of pink icing. The whirling feeling in her tummy returned.

"Millie," Dolly said as she bounded across the garden. "Follow me."

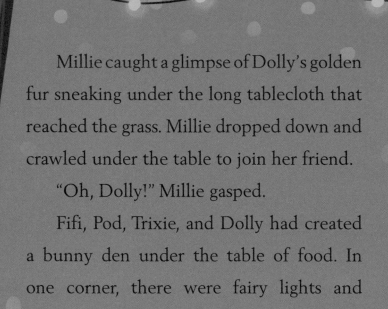

Millie caught a glimpse of Dolly's golden fur sneaking under the long tablecloth that reached the grass. Millie dropped down and crawled under the table to join her friend.

"Oh, Dolly!" Millie gasped.

Fifi, Pod, Trixie, and Dolly had created a bunny den under the table of food. In one corner, there were fairy lights and

tiny cushions from Millie's doll's house. In another, there was an egg carton that had been painted in blue polka dots and filled with snacks for the bunnies. Everything looked just like the table they were sitting under.

"What's this?" Millie asked as she looked inside a shoebox full of old wrapping paper.

"That's where we hide in case someone looks under the table," Fifi explained.

"Millie!" a voice called from the house.

"I've got to go," Millie said, hugging each bunny in turn.

"Have fun!" Dolly squealed, as party music started to play in the garden.

Millie clambered out from under the table and dusted off her dress. Mom had bought it especially for the party, and it was covered in tiny sparkly prints of ballet shoes.

"Millie, let's play!" a group of her friends from school called out.

She hurried over to find that Mom

had set up a game of Pin the Tutu on the Ballerina. It was Millie's turn. Mom tied a thick satin ribbon over Millie's eyes so she

couldn't see and spun her around. Millie clutched the pin attached to the tutu and held out her arms to try to feel for the picture of the ballerina.

"Go, Millie, go!" her friends cheered.

Millie grinned as she poked the pin through where she thought the tutu should go. Then she whipped off her blindfold, only to find that she'd pinned the tutu to the ballerina's head.

She and her friends fell down laughing when Mom took her turn and pinned the tutu to the collar of Auntie May's cardigan, which was hanging off the back of a chair.

"Time for Freeze Dance!" Auntie May

called out. "And there are prizes for whoever holds the best ballerina poses."

Millie giggled as her friends groaned. There was only one person who could possibly win: ballet-loving Millie.

Chapter 5

When the music stopped, everyone froze in their best ballerina poses. Millie stood high on her tiptoes in the *relevé* position that she had practiced with Dolly earlier that week.

And that's when she saw Sylvie! Granny's china doll was being dragged

across the garden by Adam, her
friend Samira's little brother.

Oh no, thought Millie. She
remembered she'd been playing
with Sylvie again this morning
in the living room while Mom
was busy getting the party ready. She had
meant to put the doll safely

back on the shelf in her bedroom, but she'd forgotten!

Millie broke out of her pose and ran toward Sylvie, but then stopped. Mom always said she should share her toys, especially with younger children. It was the kind thing to do.

Sylvie's neat bun began to unravel as Adam combed his fingers through her silky hair.

Millie wrung her hands. She wanted to grab Sylvie from Adam, but she didn't want to upset him. Her stomach churned so hard she felt like she had to hold it in place. Millie had to find Mom. She would know what to do.

Millie looked around the garden. It suddenly felt far too loud and far too full of people. Millie looked back at Adam, who

was still gripping Sylvie much too tightly.

Millie hurried across the lawn toward her mom, squeezing through the group of parents.

But now Mom was busy pouring lemonade for everyone.

Millie blinked hard as she felt tears in her eyes. She needed someone to help her.

And then she remembered the four little bunnies, hiding under a table.

Chapter 6

"Adam has Sylvie!" Millie cried as she dove under the tablecloth.

Fifi quickly poked her head out from under the table. "Millie's right," she confirmed.

"I need to get her back," Millie sobbed. "She's too delicate to be played with but

I don't want to upset Adam, and Mom is very busy with the party."

Pod and Trixie nuzzled into Millie's wet cheeks as she cried.

"Don't worry, Millie," Dolly said. "I have a plan."

Millie and the other bunnies looked over at Dolly, who had whipped off her tutu and was rocking back on her hind legs.

"Oh, *bunny fluff*," Fifi gasped.

"What are you doing, Dolly?" Millie cried.

"I'm going full-on rabbit," Dolly said, and bounded out from under the table.

Millie sprang out in time to see Dolly jump across the lawn and into full view of everyone at the party.

"Dolly!" Millie screeched.

Everyone turned to look at her.

"Bunny!" Adam screeched.

Now everyone turned to look at him.

He dropped Sylvie and chased after Dolly, who decided to take the scenic route around the garden. She hopped a full circuit through all the guests' legs and over the garden gnomes before darting out of sight across Mom's vegetable patch.

Millie used the distraction to rescue Sylvie. She ran toward the doll and bundled her up quickly, holding her close to her chest.

She smoothed and tidied Sylvie's hair as she made sure her favorite doll wasn't damaged. Her chest felt heavy and her

55

mouth as dry as sand as she checked Sylvie's arms and legs, and then her silk dress and slippers.

Sylvie was in good condition. She had been saved just in time, thanks to Dolly's plan. Still, Millie couldn't stop the heavy tears rolling down her cheeks as she hugged her doll tight and thought of the risk Dolly had taken to help her.

Chapter 7

As the bunny commotion in the garden died down, Millie slid back under the table and into the bunnies' den.

Fifi had gone to find Dolly, leaving Pod and Trixie alone in the den when Millie joined them.

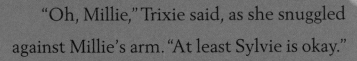

"Oh, Millie," Trixie said, as she snuggled against Millie's arm. "At least Sylvie is okay."

"But she might not have been," Millie sobbed, her shoulders slumped forward. "And it would've been all my fault. Mom is always telling me to put her away, and I always forget."

"Luckily, Dolly saved the day," Pod said.

"But who knows what could've happened to Dolly!" Millie wept. "She could have been hurt trying to help me."

"But she wasn't," Pod reassured her. "And by the looks of it, she had the time of her life running around your party."

Millie brushed away her tears with her sleeve, but she couldn't get rid of the horrible, whirling feeling that was bubbling up from her tummy.

She hung her head low. "I wish I'd never had a party."

Pod gazed up at Millie, his eyes full of kindness.

"I mean it," Millie said, trying to blink back more tears. "I could never have forgiven myself if something had happened to Dolly or Sylvie."

Millie gently straightened Sylvie's pink ballet dress. She untied Sylvie's hair and combed her fingers through it before carefully twisting it into a bun. Then she pinned the little yellow satin flower behind Sylvie's ear. Trixie helped straighten Sylvie's 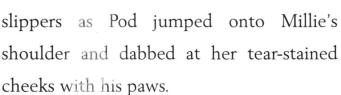 slippers as Pod jumped onto Millie's shoulder and dabbed at her tear-stained cheeks with his paws.

"I just wish everyone would go home

now," Millie whispered. "The party is too loud, and there are too many people here. It's all too much."

She looked around the den and at the warm lights and cushions the bunnies had placed in the soft grass. Under the table, away from the noise and close to Pod and Trixie, Millie felt safe.

"I'm going to stay here until everyone goes home," she announced. "I'm not moving."

Chapter 8

"You can stay here as long as you want, Millie," Trixie told her.

"And it's okay to feel upset," Pod said.

"Really?" Millie sniffed.

"Of course," Pod said. "I find noise and crowds sometimes upset me too. I get a horrible feeling in my tummy, and my chest feels tight."

"That's exactly how I feel," Millie exclaimed.

"I have a good trick that helps me during those times," Pod said. "I can teach it to you if you want?"

Millie nodded eagerly and sat down cross-legged with the bunnies.

"First, you need to shut your eyes," Pod said as he closed his.

Millie and Trixie shut their eyes too.

"Now, you need to take some deep breaths in and out," Pod said. "Imagine you are smelling a beautiful flower as you

breathe in. Then imagine you are blowing away dandelion seeds as you breathe out."

Millie took a deep breath in. And then let the breath out.

She did it a few times until she could almost smell the honeysuckle that grew around her house. As she breathed out, she

imagined she was in a meadow, blowing dandelion seeds, with the warm sun on her face and the birds tweeting in the trees above.

With every breath in and out, the sound of the party grew softer. Millie could feel the tightness in her chest and the whirling in her tummy melt away.

After five breaths, she opened her eyes and saw Pod and Trixie do the same.

"This final part is the most important," Pod said. "Find someone you love and give them a cuddle."

Millie gathered up Trixie and Pod and held them close.

"Thank you, Pod," Millie said. "I feel a lot better."

She kissed the little bunnies on their heads and stroked their long ears before placing them back on the ground.

"Now that you're here," Trixie started, "you can join in *our* party games."

Millie laughed and crawled after Trixie, who led her to the far end of the table. There, strung up on the table leg, was a picture of a bunny. Trixie handed Millie a cotton ball with a small tack on the end.

"We're playing Pin the Tail on the Bunny," Trixie said, jumping with glee. "It's your turn now, Millie."

Millie shut her eyes and reached out,

before accidentally tacking the tail on the
nose of the bunny. Pod and Trixie rolled
about on the grass, giggling at the fluffy-
nosed-bunny picture.

"We played a game just like this," Millie laughed. "But we had to place the tutu on the ballerina, and Mom pinned it to Auntie May's cardigan."

The bunnies giggled again. "That sounds like so much fun," Trixie said.

"It was," Millie agreed.

"What else did you play?" Pod asked.

"We played Freeze Dance, and we had to pose as ballerinas when the music stopped," Millie said. "I stopped in *relevé*," she added proudly.

"I bet you won that game," Pod said.

Millie's smile faded to a frown. "That's when I saw Samira's little brother with Sylvie."

Trixie placed her paw on Millie's hand. "It sounded like a wonderful party up until then."

"It was," Millie admitted. "I was having lots of fun."

She poked her head out from under the tablecloth and saw her friends playing a dancing game on the lawn.

"It's okay to go back out there if you want to," Pod encouraged her.

Seeing her friends dance made Millie realize how much fun her party had been. And now that Sylvie was safely back with her, she really did want to dance too.

Millie sat up and crawled to the edge of the table. "I think I will go back," she said

bravely. "I'll put Sylvie upstairs in my bedroom, and then I'll go have more fun."

"Go, Millie, go!" Pod and Trixie cheered.

Millie held Sylvie close and waved at the bunnies as she scrambled out from under the table. Then she waved to her friends.

Chapter 9

Mom waved goodbye to the last of the guests as Millie handed out the remaining party favors. Mom had filled each bag with a little wooden ballet doll and matching hairbands.

As soon as everyone had left, Millie rushed over to the bunny den and lifted the tablecloth. She hadn't seen Dolly since the commotion, and she was a little worried that she might not have made it back yet.

But the den was empty of *all* the bunnies. Millie looked in the shoebox too, but they weren't in there.

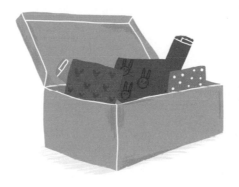

Millie hurried upstairs to look for her friends, but her bedroom was empty. There were no bunnies on the bookshelf, nor were her friends in the teddy pile.

And then her comforter slipped back.

"Happy birthday, Millie!" Trixie, Pod, Dolly, and Fifi yelled as they jumped out from under the bedsheets.

"You were hiding!" Millie exclaimed, gathering them up in a huge cuddle.

"Did you see me? Did you see me?" Dolly said as she wiggled her bottom excitedly. "I ran across the *whole* garden!"

"You did," Millie laughed. "And you saved Sylvie."

Millie placed a big kiss on Dolly's head, as the little bunny jumped out of her arms and sprang around the bedroom re-creating her daring garden run.

"Did you enjoy the rest of your party?" Pod asked Millie.

Millie nodded. "I had the best time," she said. "And I've made plans for the rest of

the holidays to see all my friends from the party."

"That sounds wonderful," Fifi said.

"It certainly does," Dolly agreed. "And it also sounds like that's *our* cue to head back to Miss Luisa's School of Dance."

"Already?" Millie said, feeling a little disappointed.

"You have lots of fun with your friends to look forward to," Dolly said.

Millie smiled. Dolly was right.

She waved goodbye to the bunnies as they climbed out of her window and hopped across the garden toward the dance school.

And then Millie smiled at Sylvie, who was back on her shelf, safe from harm and far away from little brothers.

Basic ballet moves

First position

Second position

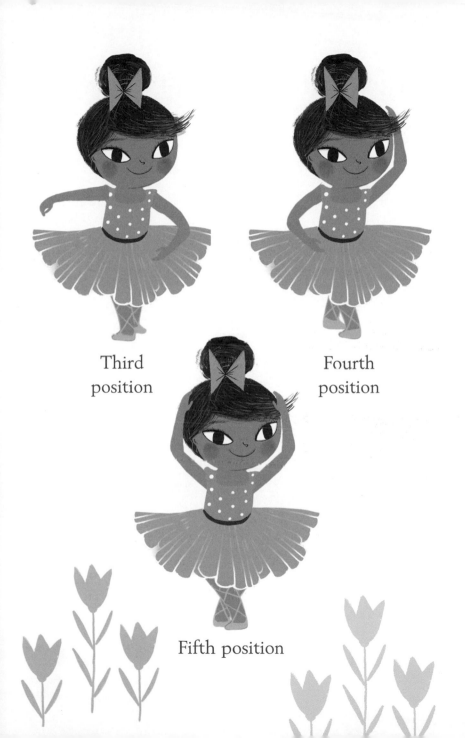

Third
position

Fourth
position

Fifth position

Glossary of ballet terms

Arabesque—Standing on one leg, the
   dancer extends the other leg
   out behind them.

Barre—A horizontal bar at
   waist level on which ballet
   dancers rest a hand for
   support during certain
   exercises.

Demi-plié—A small bend of
   the knees, with heels kept on the floor.

En pointe—Dancing on the very tips of the
   toes.

Grand plié—A large bend of the knees,
   with heels raised off the floor.

Pas de deux—A dance for
two people.

Pirouette—A spin made on
one foot, turning all the
way around.

Plié—A movement in which the dancer
bends the knees and straightens them
again while feet are turned out and heels
are kept on the floor.

Relevé—A movement in which the dancer
rises on the tips of the toes.

Sauté—A jump off both feet, landing in the
same position.

How to make bunny ears!

You will need:

- A spare plastic headband
- Card stock
- Scissors
- Crayons/glitter/anything you like for decoration
- Glue/tape
- Pen or pencil

1. Draw your bunny ears on the card stock. Make the ears a little bit longer than you want them to be.

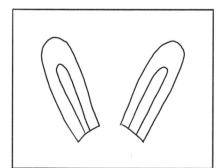

2. Decorate your ears any way you like!

3. Once your decorated ears are dry, cut them out.

4. Fold the bottom of the ears around the headband, and use tape or glue to secure.

5. Enjoy being a bunny!

Twirl and spin with the Ballet Bunnies in their next adventure!

Ballet Bunnies
The Lost Slipper

By Swapna Reddy   Illustrated by Binny Talib

Four little Ballet Bunnies.

Dolly, Fifi, Trixie, and Pod, the resident Ballet Bunnies at Miss Luisa's School of Dance, had snuck into Millie's large coat before she had climbed on board the bus from the school. There was no way they were going to miss the chance to see *Cinderella*!

As the bunnies squirmed, Millie wiggled around under the weight of the coat, hoping to hide her furry friends from Auntie Karen. Millie had forgotten the hole in her left pocket, which the bunnies were now using as a warren to travel to each other. Every now and then the coat would sag to one side as all four bunnies snuck into the same pocket!

Discover more magic in these page-turning adventures!

For the totally unique ballerina!

For the unicorn-obsessed!

For dog lovers and budding pirates!

For cat lovers and wannabe mermaids!